The Safari Challenge

Bear Grylls

Illustrated by Emma McCann

✕ Bear
Grylls

BEAR GRYLLS ADVENTURES

First American Edition 2019
Kane Miller, A Division of EDC Publishing

First published in Great Britain in 2018 by Bear Grylls, an
imprint of Bonnier Zaffre, a Bonnier Publishing Company
Text and illustrations copyright © Bear Grylls Ventures, 2018
Illustrations by Emma McCann

For information contact:
Kane Miller, A Division of EDC Publishing
PO Box 470663
Tulsa, OK 74147-0663
www.kanemiller.com
www.edcpub.com
www.usbornebooksandmore.com

Library of Congress Control Number: 2018946333

Printed and bound in the United States of America
1 2 3 4 5 6 7 8 9 10

ISBN: 978-1-61067-931-2

To the young survivor
reading this book for the first time.
May your eyes always be wide open
to adventure, and your heart full
of courage and determination to
see your dreams through.

1

HUNGER PAINS

Evie crawled ahead through a ditch full of damp, rotting leaves, then straightened up behind a tree, keeping out of sight.

"It's perfect," she whispered excitedly back to her friend Harry. "If you crawl down this ditch, the flag is only sixty feet away."

Evie and Harry were playing capture the flag. They had one thing on their minds – reaching the clearing in the middle of the woods where the flag was planted, without being caught by the boys and girls who were guarding it. They both wore an armband stuck on with Velcro. If anyone in the clearing was able to tear it from them, their turn would be over and they would become guardians too. But if they got to the flag with their armbands still on, they would win!

Evie looked back. Harry was staring glumly at the ditch. "It looks really gross," he moaned. "I don't want to get my jeans dirty. Chimp Skinnys are so expensive."

Evie sighed. That was *so* Harry, caring more about his jeans than winning the game.

But she knew there was no point

arguing with him when his mind was made up.

So instead, Evie and Harry crept from tree to tree. Both of them were crouching down by a bush, keeping very still and almost holding their breath, as a guardian stalked by.

And then there was a loud rumbling sound from Evie's stomach.

Evie's face turned a bright, burning red.

A guardian had heard. *"Intruders!"*

Evie and Harry fled, with the guardians chasing them.

"Why couldn't you just lie down in the ditch like I said?" Evie gasped as they ran.

"It's not *my* fault! Your stomach gave us away!" Harry panted. "Didn't you have any breakfast?"

Evie didn't really want to think about breakfast. All she had been able to choose was a banana and a roll. After a couple of bites she had changed her mind about the roll.

"Let's split up," she said.

"Okay. See you later."

Evie sprinted back in the direction of the ditch, two guardians closing in behind her.

4

Evie stood holding her lunch tray. All the other campers were chatting and laughing as they filled their plates. But not Evie. Hers was empty.

It had been the same at breakfast.

It was the same at *every* meal.

Camp meals were epic, and they took care of everyone's needs. Vegetarian, vegan, gluten-free, lactose-free, kosher, halal, whatever. But there was never anything that was right for *her*.

Camp food never came close to Evie's perfect meal. It was always too sloppy or too spicy, and she never knew when she might find something unexpected and gross on her plate.

So, even though she was hungry, as she stood at the front of the lunch line, she couldn't make up her mind.

By the time Evie sat down with a handful of things on her plate, almost everyone had finished. The cleanup crew were getting ready for action. She looked at her plate. An apple that looked a bit bruised on one side. A spoonful of dry-looking rice with raisins. A couple of crackers and a slice of cheese that was the wrong color. The only thing she could possibly eat was the crackers. The rest, she just knew with a guilty stab, would go to waste. She had only taken it because the leaders all insisted that she eat *something*.

The crackers were so dry they made her mouth feel like it was full of cotton. Evie wandered back into the food tent to look for the water pitcher.

The tent was empty, except for a boy called Charlie. And he was carefully dropping a stone into the pitcher. He stared at it like it was really important.

"That's disgusting!" Evie couldn't help a flash of temper. "I was just about to pour a drink!"

Charlie whipped his head around.

"Oh, sorry." He reached into the pitcher.

Evie saw what he was about to do.

"Don't put your fingers in the water too!"

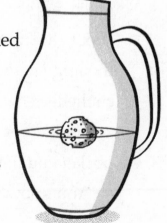

Too late. Charlie had picked the stone out of the water again.

"I could get you a drink from the sink?" he suggested as she trudged back to her seat outside.

Evie was grateful when Charlie brought her the glass. She was surprised when he sat down with her. Her meals were usually lonely because she took so long choosing her food.

They chatted a little while Evie finished her crackers, trying not to grimace too much as she swallowed. They talked about the afternoon activities. Evie had thought she would try the construction challenge.

Suddenly Charlie reached into his pocket and held out a compass.

"You know," he said shyly, "whatever

you do this afternoon, I think this might be useful."

"Er, thanks," Evie said. She took it, even though she wasn't sure why a compass would help with building things. "Do you want to swap something for it?"

Charlie shook his head.

"It's okay," he said. "Just consider it a gift." He gave a last smile. "See you at the construction challenge," he called over his shoulder as he hurried off.

Evie took her tray over to the rest of the piled-up dirty plates. As she headed for the tent exit, she checked the compass.

Oh, thanks, Charlie! she thought grumpily. The compass had five directions on it, not the usual four. And what was wrong with the needle? It kept spinning around and wouldn't rest. "Like a broken compass is going to be really helpful ..."

Evie stepped out of the tent into sunlight.

Way too much sunlight. She squeezed her eyes shut against the sudden glare.

"Whoa!"

A wave of heat swept over her. Wow, talk about a heat wave. So far camp had been mostly sunny with a bit of rain, but no one had said anything like this was coming.

Evie slowly opened her eyes.

But camp had vanished. Instead, she was standing in the middle of a vast sea of yellow-brown grass that came up to her knees.

And there ahead of her, as large as a house, staring right at her and flapping its massive ears, was the biggest elephant she had ever seen.

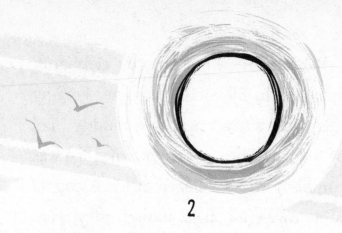

2

DON'T MESS WITH MOTHER

Evie stood still. *Very* still.

Every elephant she had ever seen in a zoo looked friendly. But this one wasn't just *looking* at her, it was *glaring*.

The elephant was about two hundred feet away, but she could still see that its dark-gray skin had more wrinkles than she could count. Then there were the two long, dirty white tusks, which were curved and pointed.

Behind it were more elephants, standing in the shade of some scraggly trees and bushes next to a muddy pool of water. They were making gentle, rumbling noises at each other. A couple of them were babies, though they were still almost as big as a car. Evie watched as one of the adults dipped its trunk into the water, then curled it back and sprayed itself. The air was so hot that everything seemed to shimmer.

None of the elephants in the pool seemed worried about Evie. But the big one was still staring at her. She knew she was in danger.

Just then, someone spoke quietly behind her.

"Don't move," murmured the man's voice. "Just stay still like you are, and don't look around. That beautiful creature staring at you is the matriarch – the chief mother of the herd. Elephants are very protective of their young, and it's her job to move to the front if she thinks the herd may be in danger."

Although she wanted to turn to see the man who had appeared out of nowhere, Evie did as he said. He sounded like he knew what he was talking about.

"Danger?" she whispered. She couldn't think what could possibly harm an elephant. They were *massive*.

"She thinks we might be dangerous."

"But we wouldn't hurt her," Evie said.

"Well, she just knows we're humans – and in her experience, humans mean trouble. There are people around who'd shoot her to take her tusks."

Evie stared at the enormous animal. What kind of cruel person could kill such an amazing creature, she wondered, just to get hold of a pair of extra-big teeth?

"What should we do?" she whispered.

"We just back off," the man said simply. "We don't turn around or make any sudden movements, but we make it very clear we're leaving. Ready? Let's go."

Evie took a step backward, feeling the long grass brushing her legs. The sun was baking hot and it felt like every part of her skin was slowly roasting.

Suddenly the elephant's behavior changed. She stopped flapping her ears and shaking her head.

Instead she flattened her ears against the sides of her head and stopped sweeping the ground in front of her with her trunk. She curled it up between her tusks.

"Uh-oh," said the man, still just as calm as ever. "She's going to charge. We can't outrun her, so just follow me and do exactly what I do…"

The elephant charged.

"*This way!*" said the man, spinning her around.

Evie followed as they sprinted through the dry yellow grass. She could hear the thunder of the elephant's footsteps behind.

Suddenly Evie tripped and the ground fell away. She tumbled down a grassy bank and gasped as her elbow scraped against the dry ground. The man took the slope with long strides. A moment later, they were both standing at the bottom of a dry ditch, gasping for air.

The matriarch elephant had stopped at the top of the slope. Her ears were flapping again and her trunk was uncurled. She threw back her head and gave a loud trumpeting blast.

"Translated, that means 'I win and

don't you forget it,'" said the man. He grinned down at Evie. "Elephants don't charge downhill. They're too heavy, so they overbalance and hurt themselves. Coming down here was the quickest way to safety."

The man helped Evie stand up while

she clutched at her hurt elbow. She looked around.

"What is this place?" she asked.

"This is a dry riverbed," he said. "Probably leads down to the water hole that you saw. In the rainy season, this place will be flowing."

That wasn't what Evie had meant. She had meant, *where am I?* And why isn't it camp? And who was this man who had appeared from nowhere and was helping her like this?

She looked at him carefully. He was tall and suntanned, wearing a battered, wide-brimmed hat, tough-looking clothes and scuffed boots. He had a backpack, and there was a knife with a long blade hanging in a scabbard from his belt.

He nodded at her hurt elbow. "May I check that for you?"

Evie nodded.

"We should get this seen to," he said, examining her grazed skin. "I saw something this way that will help."

He turned to hike up the side of the ditch away from the elephants. "Come on," he said and Evie followed. She didn't want to do anything to make the matriarch angry again.

When they got to the top, Evie slowly turned a full circle where she stood. Now that she wasn't being charged by elephants, Evie could concentrate on the big picture.

"Where am I?" she said.

"Beautiful, isn't it?" the man said. He raised his hand to shade his eyes, taking

it all in. "This is savannah grassland, right on the equator. Safari country." He held out a hand to Evie. "I'm Bear," he said, "and I'm your guide out of here. "

"I'm Evie," she said, shaking hands.

"It's nice to meet you, Evie. We've got quite a trek ahead of us," Bear said. "Are you ready for some real adventure?"

Evie looked around again.

It was so peaceful. But also it was really *big*. Who knew what other dangerous creatures might be around? Even the elephants, which she had thought would be friendly, weren't. Evie was determined to learn, which meant she needed a guide to help her.

"Sure," she said. "I'm ready for adventure. But where's everyone else?"

She and Bear were the only people she could see for miles around.

"They're a long way away," Bear smiled. "This is a place for animals. A lot of them, all locked in a struggle for survival. See this?"

He knelt down and Evie saw something that looked like a cat's footprint.

But this wasn't a normal-sized cat. This one was *massive*. The print was bigger than Bear's hand. The big central dip was shaped like a curved triangle, and the four smaller dips around it were sharp and pointed, like claws.

There were some droppings on the ground next to it too. They were the size of Bear's foot.

Evie stood up and looked around. She had a sudden urge to make sure that the owner of this footprint and these droppings was nowhere nearby. Because out here, big cats could only mean . . .

"Welcome to lion country," Bear said.

3

THE MEDICINE TREE

"Lions!"

Evie felt even more scared now, but there was something about Bear's smile that reassured her. "Don't worry, lions are usually only dangerous if they're hungry," he said. "Or protecting their young. Or if they're surprised."

"Um," said Evie, looking around. "That's not very comforting, Bear. Are they ever *not* dangerous?"

"Well, they do sleep a lot. But yes, we take them seriously. It's not just lions, though. We're several links down the food chain here. We're going to have to use our brains to stay safe and survive, just like our ancestors did."

Evie looked unsure.

"We're going to work together and be just fine, Evie," said Bear, as he set his backpack on the ground and rummaged inside.

"I've got some things that could help you on safari." He passed her a battered green hat with a wide brim. "Like this. It will stop the sun baking your brains out."

His hands went back in the bag, and he pulled out a long-sleeved shirt made from a hard, tough kind of cloth.

"And this – you can wear it over your T-shirt like a jacket. Your arms need protecting from the sun."

"Thanks!" said Evie, jamming the hat onto her head. It felt good to have shade over her eyes. As she was about to push her arms into the shirt, she paused.

"But, won't this make me too hot?" she asked.

"As long as we keep moving, we'll have a stream of air going inside our clothes and past our skin, and that will cool us down. That's why we wear

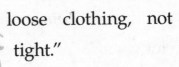

loose clothing, not tight."

Next out of the backpack came a pair of boots.

"Your feet and ankles need proper support. We've got some trekking ahead of us."

Evie winced when her sore elbow brushed against the shirt. Bear took a closer look at the cut.

"We need to deal with that, and over there is just the tree that we need."

He led her over to a tree that stood on its own, between them and a small hill. It reminded Evie of a giant clump of broccoli, with a tall trunk and a half circle of branches on top. The tree was about three times as tall as Bear, but he could reach the lowest branch. He pulled it closer and plucked off one of the leaves. The leaf was thick and shiny, almost like it was made of plastic, and its edges were jagged like a cactus.

Bear slashed the tip of his knife along the leaf. Then he squeezed it. Juices started to flow out of it.

"This is an aloe tree," Bear said. "It's one of nature's best antiseptics. There's so much animal life here that you can't leave an open wound untreated. You could end up with tetanus, or worse. Are you ready for me to put some on? I'm afraid it's going to sting."

"Okay," Evie said bravely. A bit of stinging was better than getting infected.

Bear dabbed some of the aloe juices onto the tip of his finger, then rubbed them into the cut on Evie's elbow.

He was right. It did sting, big time. But Evie breathed deeply and got through it.

"Well done, champ," said Bear as he wrapped a bandage from his pack around her elbow.

"Thanks," she said. "So, what next?"

"We need to plan the way ahead," Bear said, "so we need to get up on some high ground and take a look."

Evie rolled her sleeve back down as they trudged up the small hill she had seen earlier. Just like Bear had said, Evie could feel the air moving beneath her clothes. Even so, she wasn't exactly cool.

"Um, Bear," she said, "I'm feeling pretty thirsty."

"I'm not surprised," he said, handing her a large leather water bottle. "In this

heat we both lose water at double-quick time. If necessary we can go weeks without food, but without water we'll barely last a couple of days. That means that finding water, and saving what we have, will be one of our main priorities. Once we're up on this high ground we should be able to see signs of water nearby."

The bottle was big enough to hold a couple of liters, and Evie had to use both hands to take it. The water tasted musty,

33

but it washed the thirst away.

At the top of the hill, Evie let out a gentle *wow!* of surprise. She could see for miles and miles. The savannah seemed never-ending. She paused, thinking she could see something important.

"Is that a river?" she asked eagerly, pointing to a line that wiggled its way across the landscape in the distance.

"Good spotting, Evie. It is a river. That's great. Once we get there we'll have at least another thirty miles to go before we hit the next water source."

Evie scrunched her eyes. She couldn't see any more rivers around.

"There," Bear said, pointing at the mountains on the horizon. There was a flash of white on one of them.

"Probably a glacier," he said, "which

means there'll be melting water, and streams, and the source of that river – and where there's plenty of water, there's people. So, that's our destination. It's still early and it's going to get much hotter, so later on we'll find somewhere in the shade to camp for a bit. But for the next few hours, and then in the late afternoon, we'll just press on. We need to fix the direction we'll be heading –"

Evie remembered the compass. She had still been holding it when she was being stared at by the elephant, and it was in her pocket now. She took it out. Just four directions on it now. She squinted across the dial at the mountains.

"That's due east," she said.

"You're right, well done. That river's between us and the mountain, so if we stick to due east, we'll get to it."

Evie hesitated a little. Bear turned to look at her, and smiled. "It may take us more than a day to get there, but if you're up for an adventure we're going to be fine."

Evie took a deep breath in. "Okay," she said. "Let's go."

They set off down the hill. This side was steeper than the side they came up. Evie could feel her boots holding her feet in place on the ground. She was glad she wasn't still in her sneakers. She would have slipped on the grass and ended up on her back.

Evie was determined, but as they

walked in silence, for the first time she realized what kind of job she'd taken on.

The savannah might look beautiful, but elephants, lions and other animals lived there. And the heat was like a heavy weight on top of them.

And they had thirty miles to go. On foot.

With hardly any water.

4

PARCHED EARTH

The ground rose and fell in gentle curves beneath them as they walked. Evie and Bear followed the compass, heading due east, which mostly kept them on the low ground. They couldn't see the river anymore, but they could see the mountain. And they checked the compass to make sure they stayed on course.

"We're going to have to be careful

about water, until we find some more," Bear said as they walked. "Try to breathe through your nose, not your mouth – it'll help your body keep water in."

Bear stopped and picked up a couple of pebbles. "Here's a trick," he said as he popped one into his mouth and gave her the other.

"Put this under your tongue," he mumbled. "It'll help you salivate, which stops you feeling thirsty. The moisture stays in your body, so you're not losing any."

Suck on a stone? Evie made a face as she held it between her thumb and forefinger and studied it.

It had been on the ground. She didn't really want it in her mouth.

"Could I wash it first?" she asked. Bear

smiled back at her.

"The point is that we're *saving* water," he pointed out.

Evie remembered the lump of stone that Charlie had dropped in the water pitcher. She had been so grossed out that she'd refused to drink the water after that. Could she really put a stone in her mouth?

Her mouth was dryer than it had ever been. She was so thirsty. This was getting serious. So Evie rubbed the pebble on her clothes to make it as clean as possible. Then she squeezed her eyes shut, called up all her willpower, and put the pebble under her tongue.

It was cold and dry. It didn't taste too bad either. And soon it did exactly what Bear had said it would do. It made her mouth water, and she felt a little less thirsty.

But she was really hungry now instead. That single cracker at lunch wasn't enough to keep her going. Her stomach rumbled loudly and Bear turned to her with a smile.

"Hungry, huh?" Bear said. "We'll find food

as we go, but I've got a snack to keep us going. Have you ever tried biltong?"

"Bill who?" Evie asked.

"Biltong!" he laughed. "It's beef, treated with salt and spices. And it's how they used to preserve meat out here before refrigeration. It lasts for ages without going off, and it will replace the salt we're losing through our sweat." He held out a crumpled bag to her. "Here. It's *really* tasty."

Evie peered into the bag. The biltong looked like someone had cut up an old, dry leather belt into strips.

"Uh, I'm fine, thanks," she said.

"Are you sure?" Bear rustled the bag. "We've got a long walk ahead, and the heat will drain the energy out of us."

Evie tried hard to think of a reason not to eat the biltong.

"I'm not really sweating," she said. "So maybe I'm not losing salt?"

Bear crouched down next to her. "In this heat we're both definitely sweating, but out here it evaporates so quickly that we don't have time to feel wet." Bear put a piece of biltong into his mouth and chewed. "Mmm. Pretty good. Sure I can't tempt you?"

Evie shook her head and Bear put the bag away.

They walked on, and Evie tried to ignore the hunger she felt. She was used to ignoring her groaning stomach. She

felt the sun beating down on her. It was so hot, but at least it took her mind off her hunger.

"Vultures," Bear said suddenly, pointing at some tiny black dots that were circling in the sky ahead of them. "Let's see what they've got," he said. "There might be something for us."

Soon Evie could see a dead animal in the grass, or what was left of it. Lying on its side, the rhinoceros was as big as Evie. Its skeleton only had gray scraps of flesh left on the bones. It made her feel funny to look at it, so she concentrated on the four vultures that were feeding on it. They were big, black ugly birds, with wings like torn umbrellas.

Bear was silent for a while. He just stared at the rhino. Evie couldn't work out why. "This is why that elephant was right to fear humans," Bear said softly. "See anything missing?"

Evie took a closer look and saw exactly what Bear meant.

"There's no horn," she said, feeling just as sad as Bear sounded.

A rhino should have a massive curved horn on its nose, but this one just had a ragged stump.

Bear nodded.

"Poachers shoot

rhinos for their horns. People think it's got special powers and pay a lot of money for it. They put it into 'medicines.'"

He held up his fingers.

"They might as well just chew their fingernails," he told her, "because rhino horn is made of exactly the same stuff. Keratin."

Evie could feel the anger growing inside her. This rhino had been killed for absolutely nothing, except someone's greed.

"I wish we could do something," she said.

"You can," Bear said. "When you get home, tell everyone. The more people know about it, the more we can hope to stop it."

47

Before long they came across some elephant tracks. A wide path of grass was crushed flat, and the ground was trampled with footprints the size of dinner plates. Every few feet there was a pile of green elephant droppings, the size of soccer balls.

Evie and Bear looked up and down the trail, but they saw no elephants.

"They're probably heading for water too," Bear said. "That's a good sign."

They carried on walking. The closer they got to the river, the more Evie imagined what it might look like. How many animals would there be gathered around the fresh, sparkling water?

As soon as they reached the riverbank, the picture vanished like a burst balloon.

There were no elephants and no other animals drinking.

Because there was no water.

Bone-dry rocks lined the riverbed. When the water was flowing, it was probably fifty or sixty feet across. But now the smooth rocks were parched by the sun, with not a drop in sight.

The elephant footprints showed that the herd had just marched across the riverbed and kept going.

Bear looked up and down.

"Water might have soaked into the ground," he said. "If this wasn't so rocky, I'd dig a hole and we'd probably find some. But getting through these rocks will take more energy than it's worth."

Evie suddenly felt about ten times thirstier.

The sun was hotter than ever.

There wasn't much water left in the bottle.

This had to be very bad news.

5

PLAN Z

"Okay," said Bear. He looked up and down the riverbed one last time. "No water here, so it's on to Plan B."

Evie had to unstick her tongue from the top of her mouth.

"Plan B?"

"This way." Bear led the way back up the other side of the dry riverbed.

"Bear, we're going off course," Evie said. She didn't need the compass – she could see they were heading the wrong way. "The mountain's that way."

"You're right," smiled Bear. "We're taking a small detour to find water."

He led them back to the trail left by the elephants. "Here we are."

So, there was water here? Evie looked around. She couldn't see it.

Evie stared at Bear as he bent down and picked up one of the soccer ball elephant droppings. *What was he doing?* She almost squealed as he broke it open, showing her bits of grass and leaves all mixed up in it. The smell was revolting.

"Elephants have very inefficient digestive systems," Bear said, "but that means there's very little bacteria. In fact, fresh dung like this is almost sterile. And it's packed full of water. So …"

Bear tilted his head back, lifted the lump of dung up high above him, and squeezed. Yellow water squirted out. It trickled over his fingers, poured over his face, and went into his mouth.

"Urghh!" Evie was horrified. She'd never seen anything more disgusting in her whole life.

Bear smacked his lips and made a face.

"You know, there's a reason they don't sell this in stores," he winked.

"*That's* Plan B?" Evie gasped. "Drinking water from *elephant poop*? I'd call that Plan Z!"

Bear chucked the lump away and wiped his fingers on the ground. Then he clapped his hands together.

"And now, Evie, it's your turn."

Evie felt the world spin around her.

"Can't we get water from anywhere else?"

Bear smiled reassuringly. "This is an emergency. We're survivors, and survivors have to take what they're given. Water is life, and not having it is death. So until we find more fresh water, we're stuck with what's in the bottle, and what nature sends us. I didn't really like drinking elephant poop, but I know that my body needs the water right now."

Evie had never felt so thirsty. She knew she was getting desperate, and that not having enough water was serious.

Reluctantly, Evie reached down and broke off a small lump of elephant dung.

She tilted her head back. She lifted

the poop above her. She shivered. She closed her eyes. She told herself that she was about to take a drink of lovely, cool, clean water. And then she squeezed.

In her hand, the poop felt like a lump of damp, crumbly mud. There was a little resistance, and she could feel the water coming out.

Bleuch!

Evie forced herself to keep her mouth open and her hand up high as the water trickled into her mouth.

It was disgusting.

Eventually, when there was no more water coming out of the poop, she threw the lump away. She dried her face on her sleeve and then wiped her hands on the ground like Bear had.

He was grinning at her with a smile as

wide as the savannah.

"That's only for emergencies, right?" she panted. "Like when the nearest water is a hundred miles away?"

"Only for emergencies," Bear nodded. "I'm proud of you, Evie. It takes courage to overcome our fears. But you were great, and now we're both set until our next water break. But we'll take some with us just in case. Survivors need to take what's offered and be prepared."

Bear squeezed some more of the elephant poop water into the water bottle, and put some older, drier pieces of dung in his pack. As they pushed on towards the distant mountain, Evie hoped that there would be no more water emergencies.

The mountain was so far off that it

didn't seem to get much closer. Her legs were tired and her feet felt like heavy weights that she had to drag through the grass. The sun was getting higher and the heat was crushing. Her mouth was dry, even with the pebble still under her tongue, and she had a headache behind her eyes.

After a while they crossed more animal tracks. Bear knelt down to examine them.

"All sorts of animals here," he said. "Not just elephants this time. Antelope and eland and a few other things."

Evie knew what would attract lots of different types of animal to one direction.

"Water?" she asked eagerly.

Bear's big smile told her all that she needed to know.

Soon they could see animals in the distance. All sorts. Some Evie recognized, like zebras. Some were harder to name, like the creatures that looked like massive cows with curled horns. There were several things that looked like deer, all different shapes and sizes, with different kinds of horns.

The animals were at the far end of a huge patch of

bare earth. Evie and Bear had stopped beside a dark rock the size of a car. Evie started to walk off towards the animals, but Bear told her to hang on.

"The animals all come here to lick this, and we can too." He broke off a pebble-sized lump from the rock and handed it to her. "It's salt. After water, that's the most important thing for your body right now, and we've been sweating buckets without noticing. Salt makes your nerves and muscles work properly."

Evie took it in surprise. It looked more like black tar than the white crystals she would expect back home.

"Isn't too much salt bad for you?"

"You're right. It's all a matter of balance," Bear said. "We're designed to have a certain amount of salt in our

bodies. Not too much, not too little. This'll help us make it just right."

Evie thought of her headache and her tired muscles. If salt would make her feel better, she was all for it. She had drunk elephant dung water, so she could do this. She swapped it for the pebble. It tasted better.

They made their way cautiously towards the animals, which were gathered around a water hole the size of a small swimming pool.

None of the creatures took much notice of the two humans. Evie wondered if the animals had some kind of truce going on when they were near water. But just as they got closer, Bear stopped.

"And there they are," he said quietly. "I knew we'd meet them eventually."

He didn't point, but Evie followed his gaze. And gasped.

Beyond the water hole there was tall grass again. Sticking up above it, Evie could see a head. It had golden fur, two pointed ears, and a pair of black eyes.

A lioness was staring right at her.

6

CATS AND CAVES

The lioness yawned, closed her eyes and looked away. It was as if she couldn't care less, or just couldn't be bothered with two humans right now.

Evie remembered what Bear had said.

"I guess she's not hungry, or protecting her cubs, or surprised?" she said.

"That's right," Bear agreed. "Plus, lions like to ambush. If you can see them and they can see you, and if you stand tall so that you don't act like prey, you're probably safe." He waved a hand. "That's why everyone here is taking it so calmly."

Evie allowed herself to relax a little. All these animals knew lions better than she did, and if *they* felt safe...

Suddenly, there was a flash of black and gold. It was like an arrow, and it headed straight for one of the antelopes. The calm of the water hole vanished instantly as every animal fled in a different direction.

Bear knelt quickly and filled the water bottle.

"While the cheetah distracts them …" he murmured. He screwed the top back on. "Let's get off."

The cheetah was still chasing down its prey. The antelope was leaping around all over the place, which meant the cheetah had to swerve to keep up.

"Did you know that cheetah was there?" she asked as they hurried back.

"I thought there might be something waiting to ambush. I didn't want to rush straight in."

Bear tipped a couple of drops from a small bottle into the water. He screwed the water bottle shut and gave it a shake.

"Iodine drops," he said. "It'll make the water taste like rubber, but at least it'll be safe to drink."

Evie shot a final look back at the water hole, and was surprised by what she saw. The cheetah seemed to have given up. It slouched so that its stomach almost touched the ground. It slunk away and plonked itself down next to a large clump of grass. Something moved, and then three half-sized cheetah cubs came tumbling out.

"I thought cheetahs were the fastest animals in the world?" Evie said. "Why couldn't it catch that antelope?"

"You're right that cheetahs are the fastest at one-off sprints," Bear agreed. "Nothing can catch them or get away if they run in a straight line. But the antelope was making the cheetah use up all her strength zigzagging to follow her. The cheetah's burned-out now. She'll have to have a long rest before she tries

to hunt again. And even when she does grab some prey, she might be so tired that a hyena could come along and steal it before she takes a bite."

Evie thought about that as they walked.

If Evie didn't like the look of her food when she was at home, she could just say "no thanks." She might feel a little bit hungry, but she knew she was never going to starve. But out here it was different. The cheetah and her three kids might all starve if she couldn't catch their next meal.

Evie's stomach rumbled again. She almost regretted saying no to that biltong.

Evie thought hard about the cheetahs. She knew she couldn't do anything to help, not unless she ended up as their next meal herself. But maybe she wouldn't be quite so fussy the next time she didn't really feel like eating something that was offered.

Half an hour later, Bear said the iodine had done its job. Evie's mouth was so dry that she just wanted to glug half the bottle down. But Bear told her they must both just take a mouthful. Evie held the water in her mouth. *Ugh.* Bear hadn't been wrong about the rubbery taste.

The day was getting hotter. *Even* hotter. The sun had risen bit by bit since Evie had begun her safari, and now it was almost overhead. The heat seemed to turn the air thicker, like something they had to wade through.

At last, something solid emerged

ahead out of the shimmering
air.

Evie blinked and focused
her eyes on it. It was a pile of
boulders about thirty feet high,
one on top of the other, with bushes and
small trees all around the base.

"Shade!"

"It certainly looks like it," Bear said
with a smile. "We'll camp down for a
few hours, and then we'll press on in the
late afternoon."

As they got closer, Evie could see the
dark opening to a cave. Perfect!

What they could see of it looked empty,
but Evie realized she couldn't see all the
way to the back. It was too dark inside.
But anything that *was* in there would be
able to see *them* perfectly.

"Okay so far," Bear murmured as he checked the entrance. "But just in case …" He bent down and picked up a stone.

"Are you ready to move away quickly? If there's a family of lions in there they won't be happy about being disturbed." Then he threw the stone at the side of the cave as hard as he could, and shouted, "*Ha!*"

Nothing happened.

Bear threw a couple more stones. Still nothing.

"If there was anything with teeth and claws in there, it would be out by now," Bear said. He knelt and prodded the ground. More animal tracks.

"Lions, rhinos ... these are all the kinds of visitors we don't want wandering in while we're here. We need to build a barrier out of something."

Evie wanted so badly to be in that lovely, cool cave – but she also didn't want to be disturbed by a bad-tempered, dangerous wild animal. She looked around.

There was a tree about a hundred feet away, standing on its own. It reminded Evie of a giant mushroom. The trunk

was tall and thin. The branches were like a flat layer, much wider than the tree's height.

"Good spotting," said Bear. "That's an acacia tree, and its branches are good and thorny – let's grab a couple of those fallen ones."

Evie and Bear had to make a couple of trips to drag the branches over to the entrance to the cave, while the savannah slowly baked around them. Evie got a nasty jab in her thumb from a thorn that just went straight in, deep, before she noticed it hurting.

After that, she took a bit more care to avoid the thorns.

Bear tied his knife to the end of a stick with a bit of nylon cord from his backpack. "Just in case," he said, when he saw Evie looking confused.

Then, with the barrier of thorns behind them and the spear in front of them, finally, Bear and Evie went inside the cave. It smelled of the animals that had used it, but it was cool. It must have been twenty degrees cooler than outside.

Evie could feel all the tension draining out of her. She wanted to lie down and sleep.

"We'll give it four hours," said Bear. He pulled his bag of biltong out of his backpack. "Then we'll move on. Have a bite?"

Evie felt too tired to put up a fight. She knew she needed to eat it – even if it did look like a bit of old leather. So, before she had time to think of all the reasons why she didn't *want* to, she took a piece and put it into her mouth.

"Thanks," she mumbled.

Surprisingly, it tasted okay. Sort of sweet and salty at the same time.

They washed their biltong down with another swig of water. After that, Bear put the meat and the bottle away and then gave the backpack to Evie to use as a pillow. He lay down and put his hat over his face.

Evie gazed out beyond the thorns at the brightly lit savannah.

Everywhere she looked, the air was shimmering.

What would happen if they didn't find more water in this merciless heat?

7

EVERY MEAL'S A FEAST

When Bear and Evie stepped into the daylight again, the sun had moved low in the sky. The tops of the mountains were touched with a flash of orange.

"It'll be night soon," she said. "Shouldn't we stay here?"

"It's a full moon tonight," Bear said. "That means plenty of light to see by. We'll press on after dark for a few hours, before we finally settle down. Walking at night will help us conserve energy, and we'll move quicker than in the heat of the day. If we stay here we won't be any closer to water."

Bear was carrying his makeshift spear in one hand, the stick resting on his shoulder.

"Do you think we'll need that?" Evie asked.

Bear smiled.

"If there's plenty of light for us to see by, there's plenty for us to be seen by too. And big cats, like lions, have excellent night vision. It's like I said back at the water hole, we don't act like prey. Day or night, we walk tall, and we show we've got as much right as they have to be here. And if they still decide to pounce ..."

He lunged forward suddenly, flinging both his arms out.

"*HA!*" he shouted, loud enough to make Evie jump.

"We give them a bit of that!"

Evie laughed.

"We bluff them and make it clear it's not worth their trouble attacking us. We don't run because then they'll chase us. They're cats, after all."

The light around them on the savannah was turning deep red. Their shadows danced over the grass in front of them, slowly growing longer.

"Will we *really* be able to see in the dark?" Evie asked. She was still thinking of lions. Bear smiled.

"Oh, yes. It'll be a different kind of light, but there'll be plenty of it. And over there is probably our last chance to grab a meal that isn't biltong before the sun goes down."

They changed direction slightly to go over to a fat, strange-looking tree. It was the complete opposite of the thin acacia they had seen earlier. Its trunk was very wide. It had a few leafy branches on top of it, but they looked like someone had stuck them on as an afterthought. There were

leathery fruits, the size and shape of footballs.

"This is a baobab," Bear said. He gazed up at the branches. "We can eat that fruit if we can get it. Can you climb if I help you up?"

"Sure," Evie said. Eating new food was tricky, but climbing for food was easy.

Bear took his knife off the spear, put it back in its scabbard and gave it to Evie. Then Bear gave Evie a boost up. The trunk shot past her eyes and she was up at branch level. She cut away several of the fruits, which fell to the ground with a thud.

Evie's mouth watered. She was so hungry.

Evie hadn't ever really been

a big fan of fruit, and whatever this was didn't look too great. The skin was dry and tough. But Evie had absolutely no idea what it was meant to look like anyway – perhaps it was delicious inside.

When she had cut enough she climbed back down and gave Bear the knife. She watched as he cut the fruit into chunks. Underneath the skin, the flesh was pale and creamy. It tasted sour, like something between an orange and a lemon, and it made Evie's mouth twist. But it was surprisingly good and it filled her stomach.

"Eating just fruit will give us the runs," Bear said. "And that would be really dangerous out here – we'd lose too much fluid. So we need to eat some protein with it."

Evie assumed it would be more biltong – until Bear started poking around with his knife in the ground beneath the tree. He levered a chunk of earth away to show a bunch of wriggling grubs.

"Yes!" Bear picked up a grub between thumb and forefinger. It twisted and wriggled in his grip. It was about as thick as his finger, and its body was made up of white segments, like a cross between a plastic toy and a piece of white chocolate. "Not hairy," Bear said, studying it. "No dark spots under the skin. So it's not poisonous. If it's not poisonous, it's edible."

Then, in front of Evie's amazed eyes, he popped the wriggling grub into his mouth and swallowed it with one gulp.

"The key is to try not to bite them," he suggested as he held another one out to Evie. "Just get them down whole."

Evie took the grub reluctantly. Bear really expected *her* to eat *one of these*?

Then she remembered the cheetahs.

She was hungry. This was food.

She didn't have the choice to turn down food that she needed in order to avoid starving.

It wasn't what Evie would choose for a regular meal. But she wasn't in a regular place.

She shuddered. She didn't think she could do it. She watched Bear eat another grub.

"Perfect, huh?" Bear smiled.

Evie always tried to be honest.

"Not really," she mumbled. "I thought drinking water from elephant poop was weird. But this is something else."

Bear's smile grew bigger.

"You're right," he agreed, "there's no such thing as perfect, is there? There's just stuff you need and stuff you don't."

Evie hadn't thought of it like that.

"I suppose..." Evie was quiet. She pictured all the perfectly good food she had turned her nose up at before. "If something's good for you, why not eat it?" she said slowly. "Like this bug."

Bear nodded, and tapped his head.

"It's all up here, sport. If you think about it the right way, every meal can be a feast."

So Evie downed the grub. It wasn't nice, but she did it. She had just finished shuddering when they heard a strange sound like a laugh and a groan and a cough, all mixed up. It seemed to come out of the air. But the laugh didn't sound funny. It sounded threatening.

Bear was quickly attaching his knife back to the spear. He held it in both hands, with the blade pointing forward. That was not a good sign.

"What is it?" Evie asked quietly.

"Hyenas," he answered. "Nasty, cruel animals that could have your arm off with one bite. Stay close to me, Evie. We need to handle this situation carefully."

8

FOOD ON THE HOOF

Evie stuck close by Bear as he chose a path up the side of a low hill.

She saw them as soon as she reached the top. The three hyenas were about three hundred feet away. They had shaggy fur, long, lanky legs, and powerful shoulders. They reminded her of dogs, but they didn't move in the right way. They slunk around with their heads low, like they were embarrassed to be seen.

The hyenas were taking turns to run in and bite at something lying on the ground. They were constantly snarling and snapping at each other, letting out those chilling, laughing howls.

"I suppose it's good that they've got something to eat," she said quietly.

Bear nodded.

"Yes, everything out here has a purpose. Even scavengers. But if they saw us, they'd attack us because they'd just think we wanted to steal their meal."

"Which we don't," Evie said firmly, before adding, "do we?"

"Not yet." Bear grinned. "There's enough for everyone to share."

Evie looked at him in surprise.

"Are we scavengers too?"

"We're survivors," Bear said simply.

"Which means that ..."

"Every meal's a feast!"

"Exactly. Whatever's down there – that's our feast for tonight. We just need to be patient and wait the hyenas out."

After a while the hyenas trotted into the long grass, and their calls got farther and farther away. When Bear thought it was safe for them to come down from their hill, he made sure his knife-spear was at the ready, just in case, and led Evie towards whatever was left of the dead animal.

Soon their meal came into view. It was a zebra. Its head and front legs were still intact and covered with unbroken black-and-white skin. The rest of it was a mess. Large chunks of meat had been torn from its back legs.

Evie remembered the dead rhino they had seen, and how it had died.

"Did poachers do this too?" she asked.

"No," said Bear. "This was all done by wild animals. Several different types." Bear untied his knife from its spear handle, and knelt down by the zebra's undamaged front legs. He pointed at the back legs with his knife.

"That's where the hyenas were eating. Vultures will have pecked its stomach open and had a meal with what they found. And see how the neck is crushed? That's what lions do. The zebra will have died very quickly without feeling anything."

Bear paused, and looked closely at the bare bone at the shoulders where the lion had torn the flesh away. He smiled at something he saw, reached in and worked it from side to side before it came away, and he handed it to Evie.

"Maybe you'd like a souvenir?" he asked.

It was a tooth. A *big* tooth. It was curved and pointed, and it was longer than one of Evie's fingers. It was a dirty, brownish yellow.

"Is that a lion's tooth?" she asked. It was certainly pretty gross and stinky, but it was amazing too.

"Yup. If you spend your life with rotting meat between your teeth then you can expect major gum disease. If you ever get the chance to smell a lion's breath – try not to."

While he talked, Bear started cutting away at the flesh of the zebra's legs. Evie turned the tooth over in her fingers and then slipped it into her pocket.

Bear cut several slices of zebra meat, wrapped them in a T-shirt and put them into his backpack. Evie watched carefully. She was surprised that instead of wanting to look away, she was actually fascinated. She knew that this food was going to help her stay alive, and for that she was really grateful.

Bear tied his knife back onto his spear handle. They hadn't heard the hyenas again, or any other animal noises for that matter, but if there was something out there planning on ambushing them, Evie knew it wouldn't announce its presence by roaring in advance.

So they left the remains of the zebra behind them, and carried on walking.

The sun was setting and now the day was distinctly cooler. Evie didn't have the feeling that the air was solid now. She wasn't pushing her way through the heat.

Soon their shadows were stretched out ahead of them for several feet, and the whole world was bathed in an orange glow. The mountains ahead had disappeared into the gloom.

"We're right on the equator here," Bear said, "which means sunrise and sunset happen very quickly."

He was right. Evie took a final look back. The sun was a shimmering ball of orange fire on the horizon. A couple of minutes later she looked back again, and just the top of it was visible.

And then it was gone.

It was night, but it wasn't dark. While the last of the sun's light was fading, the stars and the moon were coming out.

The stars spread slowly across the sky until there were more than Evie could have ever imagined. The full moon was a circle of silver light, and the shadows on the ground were pitch-black. Everything else was shades of gray in the moonlight. Evie thought it was the most amazing thing she'd ever seen.

Eventually they made a camp in a dry riverbed. A tree grew right on the edge, and there was a small, Evie-sized hole underneath it, where its roots had eroded away the bank.

Bear shone a pocket flashlight into the hole. Nothing looked back at him and he looked pleased.

"Excellent. Somewhere for you to sleep, firewood and plenty of stones."

Evie wondered. "Stones?"

"What do you think would happen if we made a fire in the middle of this bone-dry grass?" Bear asked as he started to cut some sticks from the tree.

"Ah," she realized. "It would burn up half the savannah. So you build the fire inside the stones. Got it."

"That's right," said Bear. "Being a survivor doesn't just mean looking after yourself. We need to look after the environment as well."

Together they made a ring and base of stones and started to build the fire on top of them. The very first thing Bear put down was –

"Is that elephant dung?" Evie asked.

"Bingo! Every fire needs some tinder," Bear said. "Something that catches the flame and starts the fire off. This is completely dried out now, and most of it's just undigested grass, so it will burn nicely."

He built a pile of sticks on top of the

dung, then took a couple of bits of metal that hung on a chain around his neck. Bear crouched down and struck the metals together so that sparks flew. He blew gently into the base of the fire. It started to glow as flame spread through the sticks with snaps and crackles.

Bear skewered some zebra meat on a stick, but he waited until the fire was burning well before he held it over the flames.

"No one wants dung-flavored meat," he said with a wink. Evie watched the meat sizzle and brown in the heat. The smell tickled her nose, and her stomach responded. Evie imagined a perfect steak dinner, with some fries on the side, crisp and golden...

But Evie pushed the picture in her

mind away. This was the meal she had, and she was so grateful for it.

And when she finally bit into a warm, juicy piece of zebra steak, it tasted great – no need for fries, ketchup or anything else at all.

Every meal was a feast, Bear said. This truly had been a feast to end the day.

9

HUNGRY HIPPOS

In what felt like no time at all, Bear was saying, "Rise and shine!"

The world was still bathed in silvery moonlight, but the fire had burned down to nothing. Bear kicked dry earth over it to put out the last few sparks, and then said it was breakfast time.

Evie was hungry. She ate her piece of baobab fruit without hesitating. The biltong that she washed down with a

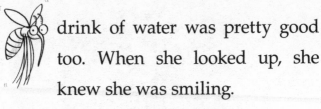 drink of water was pretty good too. When she looked up, she knew she was smiling.

"Tastes good, huh?" said Bear.

"Best breakfast ever!" Evie beamed.

Soon they were walking again, and Evie watched all the color return to the world. Orange light began to blaze between the peaks ahead of them. The air turned yellow and then white, as if the world was starting all over again.

Soon the grass seemed greener and Evie saw trees growing close together ahead of them. They were about a hundred feet tall, with graceful trunks and branches.

"Those are fever trees," Bear said. He sounded pleased. "They're a good sign because they grow near water."

And then –

"Ow!"

Something stung her neck. It really hurt.

"Ah, yes." Bear slapped at his own neck. "Mosquitoes also like the water. So we need to make ourselves less appealing to a hungry insect." He bent down and rubbed his hands in the soft earth, then smeared the dirt over his neck and face. "You need to do this too, Evie. They can't bite through dirt."

"Got it," Evie said and she quickly copied Bear.

Soon Evie recognized the smell you always got at home before a rain shower. The air was damp. The mosquitoes

were whining past more and more now, though they didn't land on her face or her hands. The muddy face mask was working.

And then Evie heard the most beautiful sound in the world.

Splash!

Water! Beautiful, clean water.

"We've definitely found water," Bear

whispered as they paused by the fever trees. "But it sounds like someone else got there first ... Tread carefully." Along with the splashing, they could hear all sorts of animal grunts and snorts.

Evie saw a wide band of silver light up ahead. They both peered through the undergrowth until they saw what was making the noise.

"Hippos!" she gasped.

There were four hippopotamuses in the river, their ears and eyes sticking up out of the water, and one standing on the far bank. Its dark, tubby body was the size of a rhino. It had to weigh a ton or more, standing on its four short legs. When it ran into the water, its body sent up a massive bow wave of water that washed all the way to the far bank.

The hippos looked harmless and pretty cute. But then one of them yawned. Its huge jaws opened wider than Evie had ever seen any animal open its mouth – at least three feet. Its fangs were almost half that, and it looked powerful enough to bite a person in two.

"These guys are very territorial," Bear said quietly, "and bad-tempered with it. We won't even let

them know we're here. They'll chase us, and they'll catch us."

Bear and Evie quietly backed away and made their way upstream, until the hippos were out of range.

Before long they came to a shallow part of the river. It was very wide and Evie could see the bottom.

"We'll be safe here," said Bear. "Hippos prefer their

water deep and calm, to support their weight."

At long last they could fill up the bottle again. Evie splashed water on herself – it felt amazing to cool down after all this time.

When they moved on, she saw some tough-looking green fruit the size of

small apples hanging from a tree.

"Are those figs?" she asked. "Our neighbor has those in their garden."

"They are indeed," Bear smiled. He gave one of the fruits a twist and it came away easily. "Ripe for plucking."

They picked a couple of handfuls. Some went into Bear's backpack and they peeled a couple to snack on as they walked.

They tasted good. *Every meal is a feast,* Evie thought. *And the ingredients for it are all around us.*

They walked a little way after that, until Bear stopped. "Decision time," he said, as they faced a fork in the river. Two streams flowed into the one that they had been following. They could see the tops of the mountains, but they couldn't see the glacier they were heading for.

"We should stick to plan A if we can," Bear said. "Which of these rivers is going to lead us to the glacier?"

"I'll check," Evie said, reaching into her pocket for the compass. She was just turning it in her fingers, trying to find east, when –

"Oh, no!" said a voice that didn't sound like Bear.

Evie looked up from the compass to see what was wrong. She froze.

The rivers, the trees, the mountains, *everything* had vanished.

Evie was back in the entrance to the food tent.

"Oh, no!" came the voice again. Whoever it was definitely wasn't Bear. And they sounded really upset.

Evie looked inside the tent. It was Harry.

Something was really wrong. His face made it look like the worst thing *ever* had happened.

"I spilled some mayo on my jeans," he said. "Can you see the mark?"

"Your *jeans*?" Evie said in disbelief. Why was he so upset? And what on earth had happened to her?

She shot another look back out of the tent door, looking for the savannah and the river.

No. Just camp.

And Harry.

"It'll never come out," he wailed.

"Mayo's got oil in it and it'll soak into the cloth. You'll be able to tell. I need to wash them before the construction challenge and there's no time to do it."

Evie started to roll her eyes. It was only clothes!

But then the thought hit her.

Hadn't her thing about food been the same? No one else had been able to understand it. She had gotten upset when people got impatient with her.

So Evie said nothing.

"I'm going to change these," said Harry as he walked past her. He nodded at the compass, which Evie was still holding. "You should bring that to the construction challenge. We might be able to use it!"

"I already have," Evie murmured as he hurried off. The compass had helped her and Bear navigate miles and miles on safari under the beating sun. But the weird thing was that despite everything she remembered, it was pretty clear that no time at all had passed back at camp.

Maybe the compass had caused an incredibly weird dream? She would think about it later. Evie shoved the compass into her pocket and set off.

10

CRAZY CONSTRUCTION

In the middle of the clearing was a large pile of boxes, wheels and ropes, as well as bits of wood, metal and plastic.

Evie was on a team with Lily, Omar, Max, Mia and Harry – who had changed out of his jeans and was now wearing what looked like a brand-new T-shirt and a pair of clean jeans.

"Okay, teams, listen up!" The leader clapped her hands. "Follow the course through the woods – it starts over there. It's marked out by flags so you can easily see it, and there'll be leaders around to keep you on track."

"Hey, Joe!" Harry called cheerfully to the next team. "The course is marked, so you can't get lost!"

"Oh, ha-ha!" Joe called back.

"He won capture the flag," Harry explained to Evie, "because he got so lost, no one could find him to capture him."

"Yeah, tell everyone," Joe grumbled.

The leader was still talking.

"To get around the course, at least one of you has to be off the ground *whenever your team is moving forward.* That includes going over obstacles. You can use anything that you find to make something to carry them. The leaders will check anything you build before you start moving. All clear? Okay, then. Construction challenge ..." She blew a whistle. *"Begin!"*

Evie's team worked hard. They dashed around, constantly giving instructions and asking for help from each other. They were a real team, everyone doing their bit. Even though they came second, everyone was smiling happily at the end. Everyone, that is, except Harry. He was staring at the thick, black mark that ran across one of his jean legs. It looked like it was oil from one of the wheels they had used.

"That's another pair of jeans ruined," he muttered.

Evie winced. She was sorry, even if she still thought they were only jeans.

She put her hand in her pocket to look for a tissue – and her fingers touched something else. What was that?

Evie stared at what she had found.

"Whoa!" Harry exclaimed. He was so impressed that he forgot his annoyance. "Is that a *tooth?*"

It was the lion's tooth that Bear had given her!

"Where did you get it?" Harry said. "Can I hold it? What animal is it from?"

"Uh … a lion," Evie murmured. She passed it to him as her thoughts spun.

The safari must have been real. She couldn't have gotten this tooth from anywhere else. The compass really *had* gotten her there, and gotten her back too, before anyone noticed. It really had been useful.

She pulled out the compass.

"This is pretty cool too," she said. "Why not take it?"

Harry reluctantly gave the tooth back to her, and took the compass.

"Uh – right?" he said. "Thanks. Not sure it's as cool as a lion's tooth …"

"Maybe you'll see," Evie said. She smiled. "Just consider it a gift."

The End

Bear Grylls got the taste for adventure at a young age from his father, a former Royal Marine. After school, Bear joined the Reserve SAS, then went on to become one of the youngest people ever to climb Mount Everest, just two years after breaking his back in three places during a parachute jump.

Among other adventures he has led expeditions to the Arctic and the Antarctic, crossed oceans and set world records in skydiving and paragliding.

Bear is also a bestselling author and the host of television programs such as *Survival School* and *The Island*.

He has shared his survival skills with people all over the world, and has taken many famous movie stars and sports stars on adventures – and even President Barack Obama!

Bear Grylls is Chief Scout to the UK Scouting Association, encouraging young people to have great adventures, follow their dreams and to look after their friends. Bear is also honorary Colonel to the Royal Marine Commandos.

When Bear's not traveling the world, he lives with his wife and three sons on a barge in London, or on an island off the coast of Wales.

Find out more at **www.beargrylls.com**